To Devika, My little sister

# Poetry Notebook
## of a
# Teenage Girl

*A Poetry Collection from post-covid world*

Poems and Illustrations by

# Ishil Sibal

# Contents

# Acknowledgements

First and foremost, I would like to acknowledge that I was supposed to be studying for my First Terms instead of writing this!

Now to present my thanks - firstly, I would like to thank my biggest behind-the-scenes helper, editor, and emotional support - *my mother.*

Next credit goes to my family, and to my friends & my teachers - old and new, for encouraging me to write and for shaping me as I am today.

Special shout out to my school's English teachers – Ms. Shraboni Ghose and Ms. Anudeep Kaur for encouraging me and for reading my poems.

And most of all, I would love to thank *You, the Reader* for taking the interest and time to read my poetry collection.

# Preface

Some people might wonder, why a 13-year-old girl would ever write and publish poems?

What problems, thoughts, and responsibilities could a school-going child have?

I believe the people who think this way have perhaps forgotten their childhood. In our contemporary society, childhood has a facade of being a stage where life is all sunshine and rainbows.

In reality, we face challenges and have deep thoughts about various topics discussed in this collection. As we grow older, we tend to minimize the complexities, thoughts, and challenges faced by our younger selves.

Anyone's life isn't as simple as it may seem from afar; through this poetry collection, I present to you the vast spectrum of thoughts from an adolescent mind.

Most of the poems in this compilation held in your hands were a result of a 21-Day Poetry Challenge that I did with my mother to combat the boredom of Covid lockdown days. In this challenge, my mother and I had to write one poem each day on a random topic and share our poems with each other on the last day. And I admit that I procrastinated and wrote three poems on the very last day!

To my peers, I hope you find your own meaning in some of these verses.

To the elders, parents, and teachers, I hope the poems take you on a walk down the memory lane to your teenage years so you may better understand the feelings of today's adolescents.

Love,

Ishil Sibal

*Prose or verse;*

*when recited,*

*can create an entire universe*

*of worlds ignited by imagination.*

*Thus, the birth*

*of creation*

*is bringing you towards her hearth.*

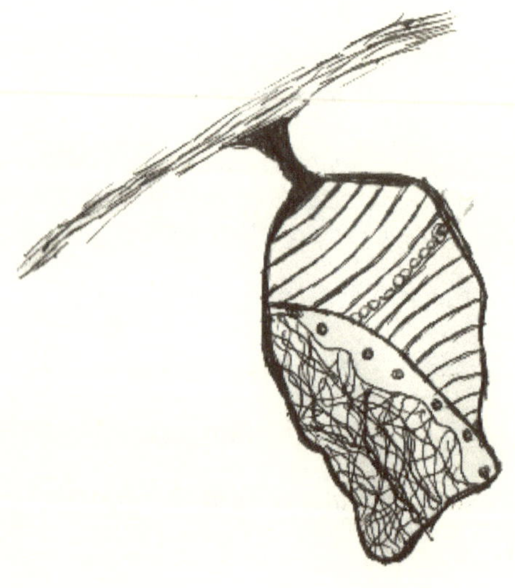

# Caterpillar

Beauty takes time
This wisdom shows itself when you seek
Born, one is a blank, waiting to be filled.
But context in a blank is the key,
For there is no answer without question,
Nor is there any one correct answer.
Before a brown caterpillar transforms
into a gentle fly,
It has to feed.
Before calling oneself wise, one should revise.
But to bring forth change, only will and
clues shall help.
When in a chrysalis, one needs to dissolve to
form again.
To sit in silent contemplation hand in hand with
patience.
For if one is not patient, wings wont dry,
Then, they won't fly.
When near a goal, instead of rushing, bask in the
closeness of your success
Take a moment to think, to blink, be one of the few to
see the view.
Then walk in confidence, and discover more to know
Learn not only upon reaching but, on every chance
you get in order to grow.

# Meek Moon

The shape of the crescent
Makes me resent
turning on any light.
Oh, ever so bright
Shining through the night
Changing shape
dancing around here and there
Since the street lights blare,
Even through my glare
You, oh crescent unable to show
how you shrink, how you grow
how you fall, how you rise,
How could they ever think,
Creatures like mice
Could ever reside on such a beauty like you.
To ever think you were made of cheese,
Oh, please!
And whenever I am blue,
I shall think of you.

# Deepness of death

Through dark depths
Reach out the reaper's hand
She was misunderstood
For she was only doing good
Separating souls from a lifeless corpse
Comforting the poor thing
For her, life is a more blink
Guiding the child to his heaven.
Consoling the un-consoled
Helping the helpless
Showing, Shadows do share
And do care
There is depth in darkness
A kind that light does not possess
That shade can be welcomed
When in summer's lengthy might
There is beauty, elegance, and grace through the
night
diving into darkness
Is sometimes better than looking at the light.

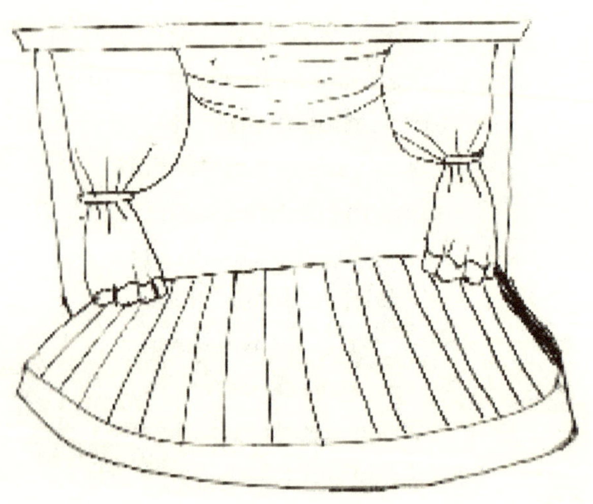

# Stage Sage

I was terrified,
Butterflies filled my stomach.
But I took a deep breath and finally stepped on stage.
My anxiousness was justified,
For t'was just my luck
My audience took me for a sage.
Hundreds of thousands here to listen,
Blaring lights enough to make my eyes glisten,
Lines of my speech swirling in my head,
Blurry and indistinct were my thoughts,
But with one I held on;
I had learnt and I had read
I could speak about lots.
Slowly but surely all my fear was gone.
I embraced the crowd, full of hopeful eyes,
Waiting, as knowledge was their prize.
A gentle trickle of words flew
Pouring out of my heart
And, as their knowledge grew,
It tore my doubts apart.

# Fake it 'till you make it

And so, I fake a Smile
No one knows me that well
To tell that it ain't real
Make it believable
Master the art
lie with your very eyes
Posture,
It matters, keep the smile seemingly real
don't let anyone see the real you
Build a dam.
It broke.
Fix it.
In a way that it blocks none
Make it believable
Faith in Me, myself, and I
A fraud
Look this topic ain't that broad,
It's a lane, full of pain
That you really do not ever wanna cross.

# Competent Communication

Inked in different hues
About reds, about blues,
Some about me, some about you,
Sharp as knife
Cold as ice
Or maybe, quite nice,
Smooth as sand,
Or hard as land,
Depends if manned.
To vocally express, one does not need to impress.

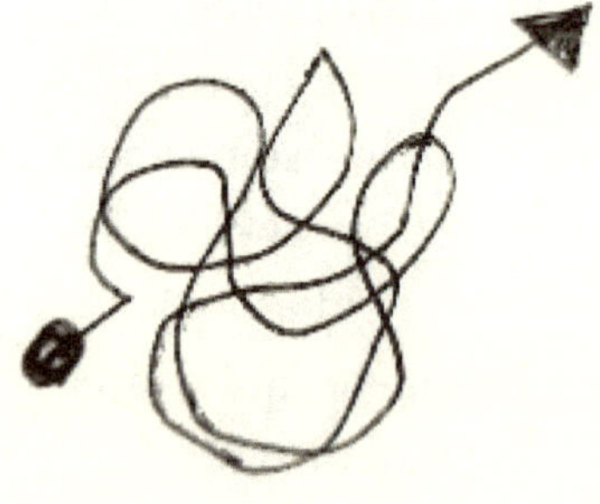

# CHaOs

Running in circles
Up a table, down a stair
Shouting, screaming, without a care
Some slow as turtles
Other fast as hare
Yet no one knows all their gears
In a class of adolescents
All ranting out their silly vents.
The teacher standing, head in hands
Stumping down upon her chair,
Students, doing all they dare,
Sometimes life just ain't fair.

# A Bookworm's Anthem

Ruffled pages
Rivers of knowledge
When they end,
My mind rages
Down by a bend
fighting to fend
Or trying to defend
Or maybe just a conversation
about a railway station
Books have me booked
looked or un-looked
Read and Re-read
'till my eyes bleed
about musts, about greed
about peace, about a dream
no matter what they seem
In my eyes they gleam!

# Fish of flight

Wish to be weightless
Fleeting, fluttering
What other greatness?
What else could exist
On Earth our planet,
In the midst of nothing and bliss.
Who could resist?
A world upside-down
Fish in flight
Birds that bathe
Bees on knees
Most of all,
Human Beings
not hunting,
nor hunted.
not starving,
but saving.
Not destroying,
but making.
Truly, in a world upside-down,
Plants would wear the crown!

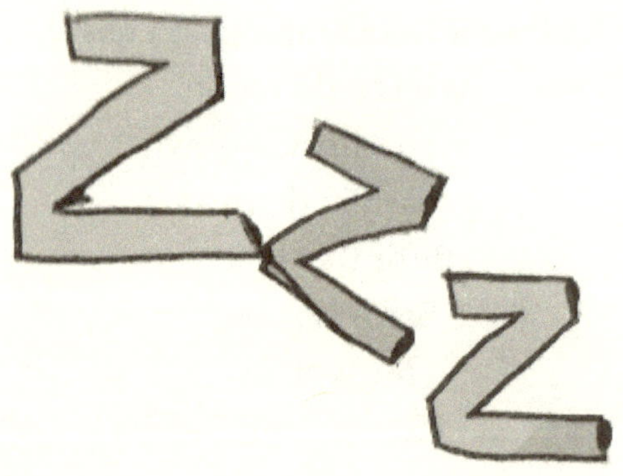

# SLEEP

Sleep is the most important deed
That one needs to pay heed
As, if not complete
One will have to make ends meet
To get through a day
And one just may
Sit on the bed and lay
Throughout that day
Thus rightly proven,
Sleep
is a requirement
To live life in all its enjoyment!

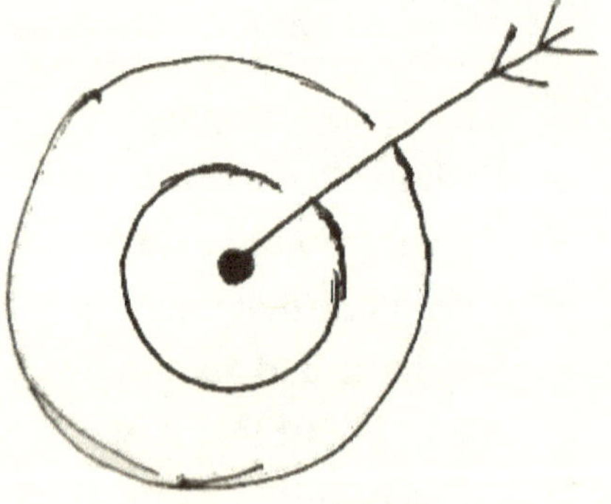

# Goal

The goal our soul does yearn
When upon one climbs Greed
And his accomplice Pride
Down to its own demands they lead
A being to its downfall
Beware of the Drunk joy of Success
As much as the destruction of Failure
For on both one can overdose
But from every rise and fall one must learn
Learn to earn more than money
Learn to earn wisdom.

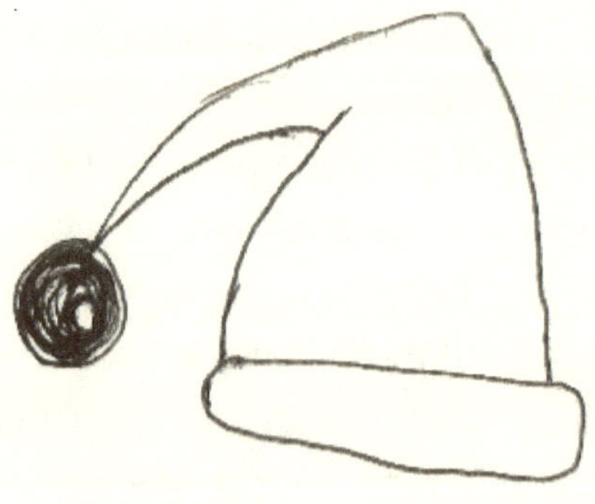

# Night of joy

In this month of Merry
Bells a'ringing,
All are cheery,
Joy in the soul very
Children watching the clock dingin'
Out come people once weary
To conversing and joyously jumping
Anticipation's tickets have sold out
Up in the sky
Oh, look Santa's sleigh
When it's all over the innocent child begins to pout
Hearts of gold
All new and old
Roaming the freezing streets
'till their heart has pumped their last beats
The season's joy shall last
May all have a blast!

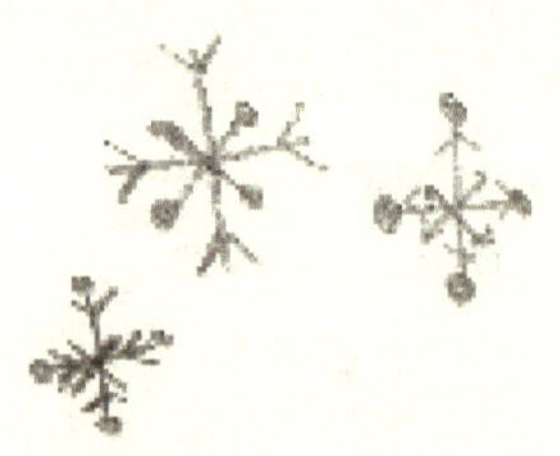

# Cold

When comes Winter's wicked reign
It can sure be a pain
layers upon layers
Dressing up can get really boring
Days so short
and Nights so long
Yet you don't get to sleep along
Winter can come and go
In some places it even snows
Make a snowman, use a bow
At night when all the stars glow
they light up all the snow.
Is faced
by the unfortunate
Human Being.

# BLANK

Unknowingly,
Unseemingly.
When beyond comprehension
Comes with
No recognition
It is no myth
One knows not what to say
They draw a blank
We just may
end this distorting disarray
And peacefully agree
That
An unpleasant situation

# My Muse

**(Ode to Up bringer)**
Knitted eyebrows
eyes filled with determination,
lips perched against one another,
Moments where
Tensed eyebrows relax
eyes close blissfully unto a sea of satisfaction
Crushed lips sigh in pure peace
Oh Ma, my muse
Why must you worry so?
Yet in the moments your motherly love seeps through
A goofy grin splattered on your face
Or
The seriousness at our silly
The pout that plays
When playfully disappointed midst a game
The anger flickering on your features
Only to be doused by a flame of love
Your love for listening
To me, to music, to anyone who is close to you
Is truly mesmerizing.

# Rainfall

Droplets tumbling down to Earth.
Petering-pattering in the mud
Children Splashing, full of mirth
Tea in my hand, filled in a mug
Walk around a veranda
filled with Shrubs.
The aroma of Soil
in the drizzle
More than a meek bristle
Potent in the air
Still standing somewhere near
Drenched from head-to-toe
Rain changing direction with Wind's every blow
Pouring to raining,
Raining to drizzling,
Drizzle to drops,
Then it all stops.

Name

# Names

Life is but numerous occasions
And moments piled together in heaps
Bound by the ties of our consciousness
Unto the deep unknown of our mind.
The heaps, organised or not, are
All our physical being possesses
Out of the many moments,
Oneself is addressed
By mere letters jumbled to signify them
One responds to that sound
That particular order of letters,
As though the sound is them
When one embraces that sound,
and acknowledges it,
The sound becomes a name.

# Home

A four-walled hut,
a building if one must,
a house full of dust,
Or a tiny little nut,
Any can be a home.
Home is not a house
For house is a box
With a roof and four walls
In which one can survive
A home is a place of security
and loneliness can't breach there
even with an army.

# Birthday Wish

If life is a trek
Faith, a vehicle;
On a path filled with
Shadows and sunlight,
Thorns and flowers.
To live, laugh and learn in life
Is the best thing to do.
Even it is a bit out of the blue,
Happy Birthday to You!

# A New Year

Clock ticking 'till midnight
One second isn't valuable 'till it is.
When the clock strikes twelve,
A year has changed,
So has the day,
As well as the hour
And the minute
This, the power of a second
Sixty in a minute
utilize it.

# The language of English

Pronunciation is a pain
All efforts may go in vain
To understand this language
which is beyond a common human
To fully for comprehend
Exceptions within exceptions of exceptions
using 'that that' in a sentence
can truly cause a rampage
Inside my brain!
Why a gaggle of girls as well as geese
group of boys instead of
'gaggle' of guys!
Near, tear, gear, dear and 'bear'
Tear and tear are same yet not
dear and deer are different yet not
a goose, then geese
Make me understand,
Please!

# Rise

Rise up to the top,
As far as an eye can see.
limitless sky; your stop
Touch the Clouds but do not let your head into them
Let your roots be Rooted as they were
Deep unto the ground
Always and Forever
For the world is round
With not an end nor a beginning
A timeless journey,
Never-ending.

# Our Beautiful Nation

The diversity in our nation
Is a beautiful creation
North, South, East or West
The ties that connect us are the best
75th year of Independence
Free from the British dependence
As freedom came by,
India is now soaring in the sky
Development at its test,
No need to follow the West.
We learn to love and learn to respect
We always learn not to neglect.
We have one country and we all her kids
Bound with the ties of tradition and relation
Full of a unified yet diverse mix.

# Practice

Precision takes practice.
The beat of a song,
A right or a wrong,
The sharpness of a step,
Or the timing of a cleverly placed clap;
The precise key of a piano,
Or the string of a guitar,
Precision is a thing
That one must perfect,
Then practice to protect the perfection.
For, precision takes perfection
And perfection takes practice.

# Contradicting Conclusions

**I**

Don't you sometimes wish
To break free
Of these chains that hold you?
To become who you were instead of
Who you turned out to be
To whisper all the things you thought
But were never bold enough to speak?
To create words so wise
That people never forget?

**II**

Am I a social creature
Or
Am I a creature of isolation,
Here only to bring solace to others?
Am I a creature of my own,
Or a creature for someone to own?
Where will all this education get me
If
Information is also the death of me?

**III**

Are the fetters holding me
For my safety?
Or for the safety of the ones near me?
Are the fetters even restrains
If they don't harm me?

# People Never Forget

People never forget
Make one wrong choice
In a sea of right ones
Your sea is forgotten.
But if you don't have a sea,
Only a Pond,
'The wrong choice' doesn't difference much a make.
People never forget.
Though they are easily misguided,
Manipulated.
Misinformed.
Convinced.
People never forget.
If they hear it,
They believe it.

# More Acknowlegments...

I would like to offer my gratitude to the poetry book - **Firefly Memories** written by Ms. Jonaki Ray - for getting me into the headspace to compose the last two poems in this collection – *Contradicting Conclusions* and *People Never Forget*.

I would also like to thank my English teacher, Ms. Preeti Attree for challenging me to write the poem – *Our Beautiful Nation*.

The poem - *My Muse* was written for (in case you haven't already guessed) my mother. One evening, she was writing a poem with a puzzled expressions on her face, which inspired this poem.

The poem - *ChaOs* was written whilst in the middle of a particularly chaotic lunch break in school that involved quite a lot of … well chaos. I hope I don't get in trouble with my teachers for saying this!

The poem - *Birthday Wish* was especially composed for my Maasu – Mr. Nalin Rawat who always enthuses me with a spirit of adventure.

I would also like to thank Ms. Geetika Saini, who is a published author herself, for her kind guidance through the publishing of my debut book.

I would like to thank my uncles and aunts, notably Mr. Gaurav Sharma, Dr. Divya Sharma and Mr. Saurabh Sharma for their valuable feedback, and to my grandparents for encouraging me.

I want to thank my friends from Bengaluru – Shragvi Panda, Aarna Srivastava, Soumya Pareek, Yashasavi Singh, Dhaya, and Aanya Rai. Next credit should go to my friends from Gurugram – Saanch, Adwika Choudhary, Vaani Sharma, Gauri Bhatia, Riya Bhatt, and Kanak Bisht. Also, I would like to offer my gratitude to my friends from my current school – Anya Kumar and Radhika Kumari. It is impossible for me to include every single name of all the friends who have encouraged me through writing of these poems, my sincere apologies to the names that might have unintentionally missed.

This book could not have been shaped the way it is today without dedicated efforts from the team from Notion Press, notably Ms. Shwetha M, Ms. Sayoni Ganguly, Ms. Puja Chand Deupa and many others in their editing, publishing and designing team who have worked tirelessly on this book.